THE MILLIONTH EGG

BERNICE MYERS

THE MILLIONTH EGG

A TRUMPET CLUB SPECIAL EDITION

Published by The Trumpet Club
666 Fifth Avenue, New York, New York 10103

Copyright © 1991 by Bernice Myers

ISBN 0-440-83048-6

This edition published by arrangement with Lothrop, Lee & Shepard,
a division of William Morrow & Company, Inc.

Printed in the United States of America
March 1993

1 3 5 7 9 10 8 6 4 2
DAN

To the rest of
the chickens
in the barn:
Barbara
Carol
Donna
Edith
Joanne
Jackie
Nancy
Peggy
Shannon
Sandy
Valery

The chickens were all excited. Any time now, one of them would lay the one millionth egg! They were getting ready to celebrate with a big party.

Elaine was in charge
of counting the eggs.
"999,996!" she called.
"Four more to go!"

"Where shall I hang
the balloons?"
Judy asked.

"Around your
tail feathers!"
said Ceil.

The chickens
worked hard and fast
to be ready in time.

What goes ha-ha-ha-ha-ha-ha-ah-PLOP?

Can we have
chocolate cake
with ketchup?

A chicken
laughing its head off!
You asked me that
yesterday.

How do you spell
stupendous?

"STOP EVERYTHING!"
Rhoda shouted
as she ran
into the barn.
"There isn't going
to be a party!
The farmer
is tearing down the barn.
He's building a restaurant,
and we all have to
LEAVE!"

The chickens couldn't believe what they heard.

"I tried my best,"
said Rhoda.
"I promised him
we'd lay three eggs
every day
instead of one.
Perfect ones.
Without cracks.
But nothing I said
would change
his mind.
So start packing."

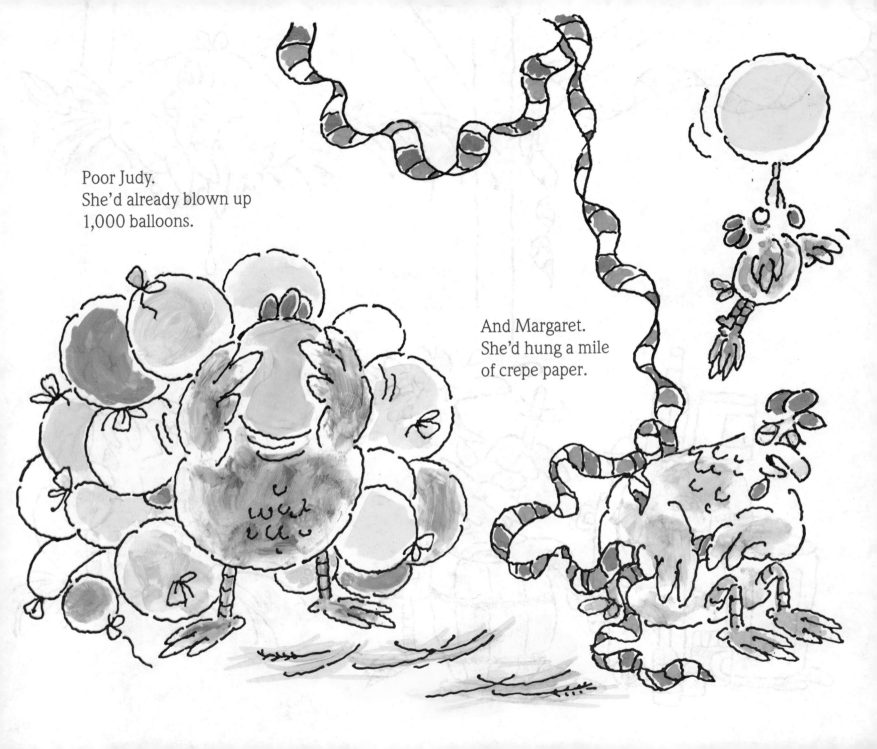

Poor Judy.
She'd already blown up
1,000 balloons.

And Margaret.
She'd hung a mile
of crepe paper.

Ceil had made
105 gallons
of punch
from a secret recipe.

We were
happy-go-lucky chickens.
Not a care
in the world.

Who was happy?

"I think
I'm going to have
a headache,"
said Mila.
"We worked so hard
all these years.
Some thanks we get.
Good-bye. . . .
Good luck. . . .
Nice to have known you. . . ."

Monica sighed.
"It's the old-age home
for me."

"At least
we won't have to
lay eggs
anymore,"
said Judy.
"Now I'll have time
to learn
horseback riding."

"Horseback riding!"
Ceil had to laugh.

But not Mila.
She was too upset.
"Who knows where we'll
be sleeping tomorrow?"

Rhoda knew
something had to be done.
And soon!
No problem
had ever been too hard
for her to solve before.
When Ceil and Judy
had claimed
the same egg,
hadn't she
divided it in half?

And when they had decided
to give up laying eggs
to do TV commercials,
hadn't Rhoda
talked them out of it?

I'm so nervous.

I can't stand the tension.

What to do?
What to do?
Rhoda tried to think.
The chickens
continued to chatter.

999,998.
Two more to go.

"I HAVE IT!"
Rhoda suddenly shouted.
"I'll write a play."
And she disappeared
into a corner
of the barn.
The chickens
were beside
themselves.

Write a PLAY?

A PLAY?

NOW?

"Rhoda
must be losing
her marbles,"
said Margaret.

"Either that,"
said Monica,
"or she's smarter
than we think."

"At least
if we leave
I won't have to hear
Ceil snore
anymore."

"Who said I snore?"
said Ceil.
"I never snored
in my life!"

"How would you know?"
said Mila.
"You're always
sleeping."

Then the chickens
fell silent.

999,999.
Only one more
to go.

"IT'S FINISHED!
THE PLAY'S FINISHED!"
Rhoda waved
a stack of papers
in the air.
"I call it
CHICKEN FEATHERS."

The chickens
rehearsed the play
over and over.
When they had
rehearsed enough,
Rhoda invited the farmer
into the barn.
Monica
opened the curtains.
"It's not going
to work.
I just know
it's not going
to work,"
she mumbled.

Baby Olivia
held up the sign.
"Let the play
begin,"
said Rhoda.

CHICKEN FEATHERS

Starring:
Ceil
Judy
Elaine
Mila and
Margaret

and the Barn Players

I'm tearing down
the barn.
You chickens
will have to leave.

But, kind sir,
we have
no other place
to go.

The barn
is the only home
we've ever known.

Our children
will starve . . .

The old chickens
will surely die . . .

And the rest of us
will be lost forever. . . .

When the play
was over,
the only sound
in the barn
was the farmer's
sobbing.
"I promise
I'll never sell
the barn.
Never!"
The chickens cheered.

They cheered again
when Ceil laid
the millionth egg.

And at last
they had their party.

A few weeks later,
the chickens and the farmer
opened a small restaurant.
Rhoda was
the hostess.

Step right this way,
please.

THE
EGGS-press
CAFÉ